HIROSHIMA NO PIKA
Words and Pictures by Toshi Maruki

Lothrop, Lee & Shepard Books   New York

That morning in Hiroshima the sky was blue
and cloudless. The sun was shining. Streetcars had
begun making rounds, picking up people who
were on their way to work. Hiroshima's seven rivers
flowed quietly through the city. The rays of the
midsummer sun glittered on the surface of the rivers.

In Tokyo, Osaka, Nagoya, and many other Japanese cities there had been air raids. The people of Hiroshima wondered why their city had been spared. They had done what they could to prepare for an air raid. To keep fire from spreading, they had torn down old buildings and widened streets. They had stored water and decided where people should go to avoid the bombs. Everyone carried small bags of medicine and, when they were out of doors, wore air-raid hats or hoods to protect their heads.

Mii was seven years old and lived in Hiroshima with her mother and father. She and her parents were breakfasting on sweet potatoes, which had been brought in the day before by cousins who lived in the country. Mii was very hungry this morning, and exclaimed about how good the sweet potatoes tasted. Her father agreed that they made a delicious breakfast, though they weren't the rice he preferred.

Then it happened. A sudden, terrible light flashed all around. The light was bright orange—then white, like thousands of lightning bolts all striking at once. Violent shock waves followed, and buildings trembled and began to collapse.

Moments before the Flash, United States Air Force bomber *Enola Gay* had flown over the city and released a top-secret explosive. The explosive was an atomic bomb, which had been given the name "Little Boy" by the B-29's crew.

"Little Boy" fell on Hiroshima at 8:15 on the morning of August 6, 1945.

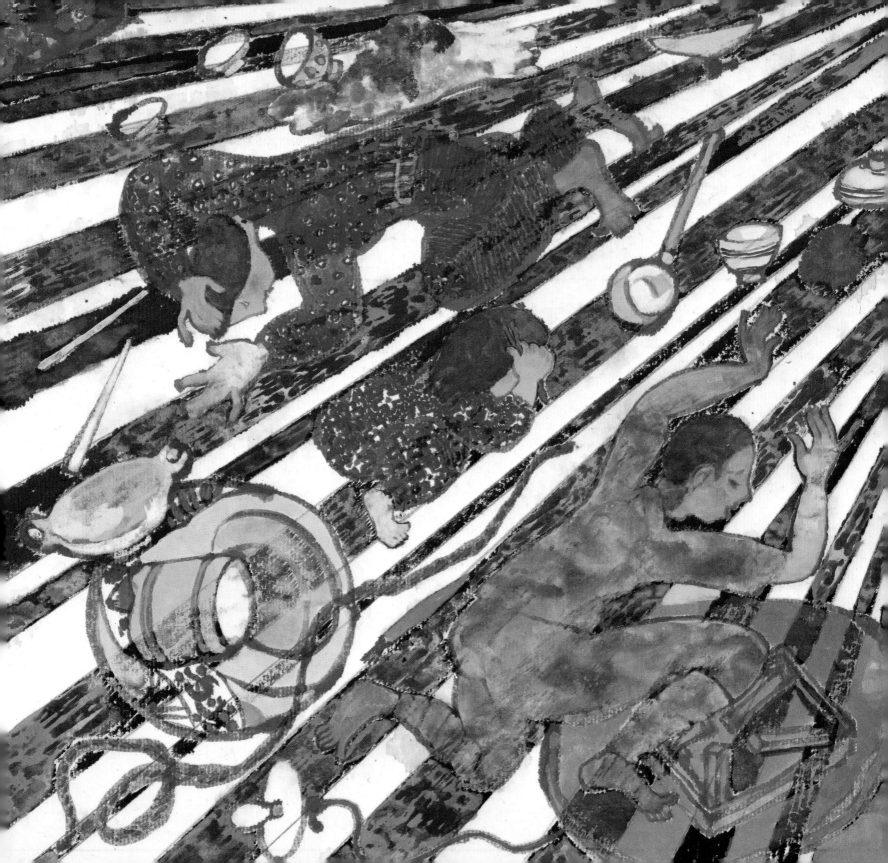

Mii was knocked unconscious by the force of the Flash, and when she woke up everything around her was still and dark. At first she couldn't move, and she heard crackling sounds that frightened her. Far off in the darkness she could see a red glow. Her mother's voice penetrated the dark, calling her.

Mii struggled out from under the heavy boards that had fallen on top of her. Her mother rushed to her and drew her close and hugged her. "We must hurry," she said. "The fire...your father is caught in the flames!"

Mii and her mother faced the fire and began to pray. Then Mii's mother leaped into the flames and pulled her husband to safety.

Mii watched as her mother examined her father. "He's hurt badly," she said. She untied the sash from her kimono and wrapped it around her husband's body as a bandage. Then she did something amazing. She lifted him onto her back and, taking Mii by the hand, started running.

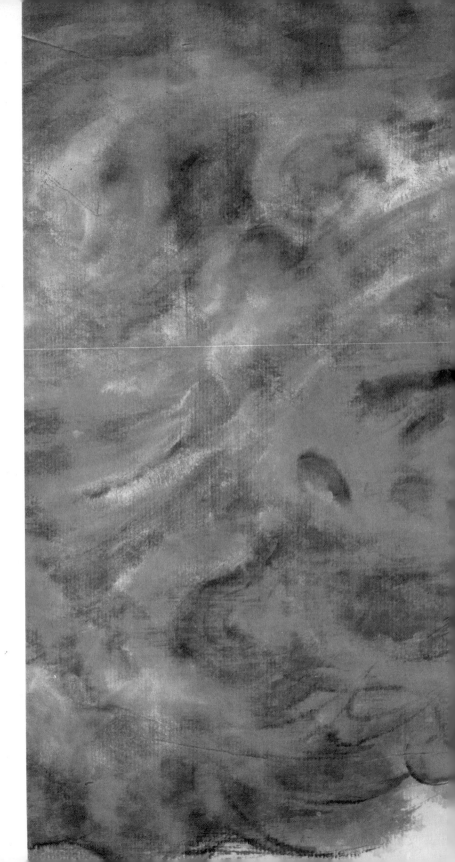

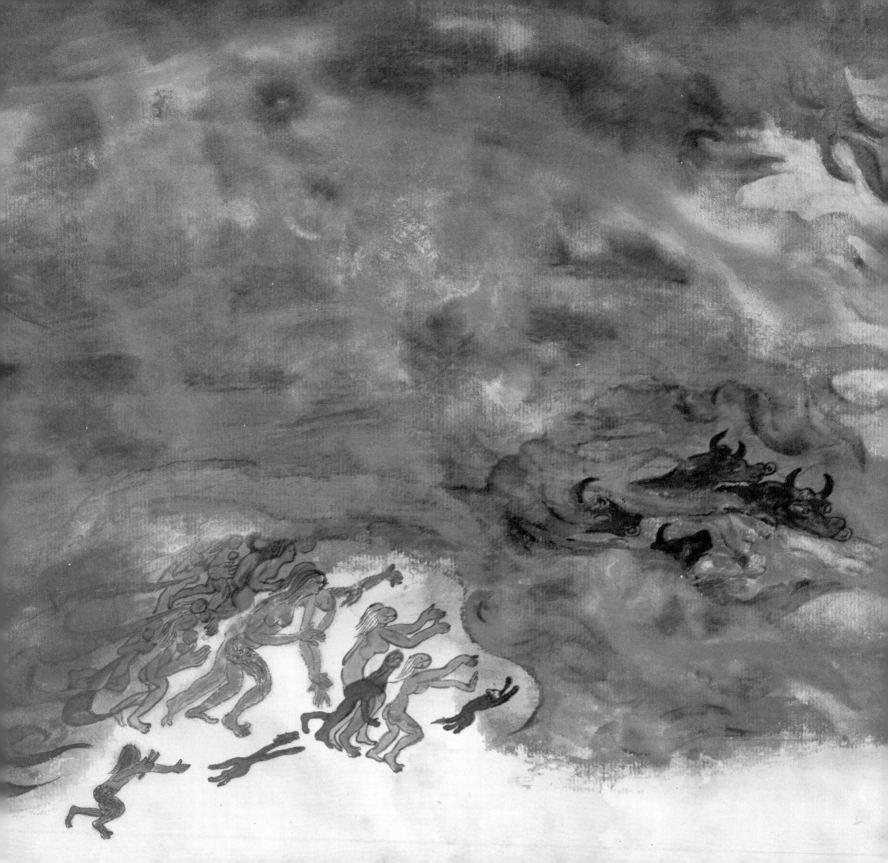

"The river. We must reach the river," Mother directed.

The three of them tumbled down the riverbank and into the water. Mii lost hold of her mother's hand.

"Mii-chan! Hang on to me!" her mother shouted.

There were crowds of people fleeing the fire. Mii saw children with their clothes burned away, lips and eyelids swollen. They were like ghosts, wandering about, crying in weak voices. Some people, all their strength gone, fell face down on the ground, and others fell on top of them. There were heaps of people everywhere.

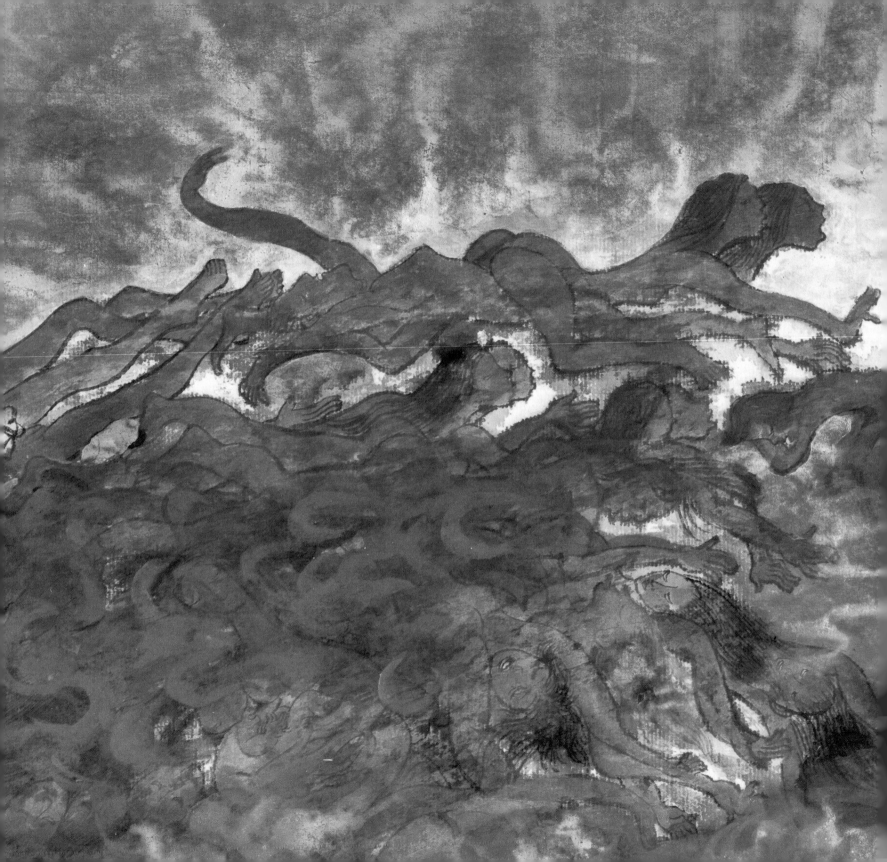

Mii and her mother and father continued their
escape and crossed another river. When they
reached the far bank, Mii's mother put her
husband down and collapsed on the ground
beside him.

Mii felt something moving past her feet. Hop...hop....
It was a swallow. Its wings were burned, and it couldn't
fly. Hop...hop...
She saw a man floating slowly down the river.
Floating behind him was the body of a cat.

Mii turned and saw a young woman holding a baby and crying. "We escaped this far and then I stopped to feed him," she said. "But he wouldn't take his milk. He's dead." The young woman, still holding her baby, waded into the river. She waded deeper and deeper, until Mii couldn't see her anymore.

Mii turned and saw a young woman holding a baby and crying. "We escaped this far and then I stopped to feed him," she said. "But he wouldn't take his milk. He's dead." The young woman, still holding her baby, waded into the river. She waded deeper and deeper, until Mii couldn't see her anymore.

The sky grew dark, and there
was a rumble of thunder. It
began to rain. Though it was
midsummer, the air turned
very cold, and the rain was
black and sticky.

Then a rainbow arched
across the sky, pushing the dark
away. It gleamed brightly over
the dead and wounded.

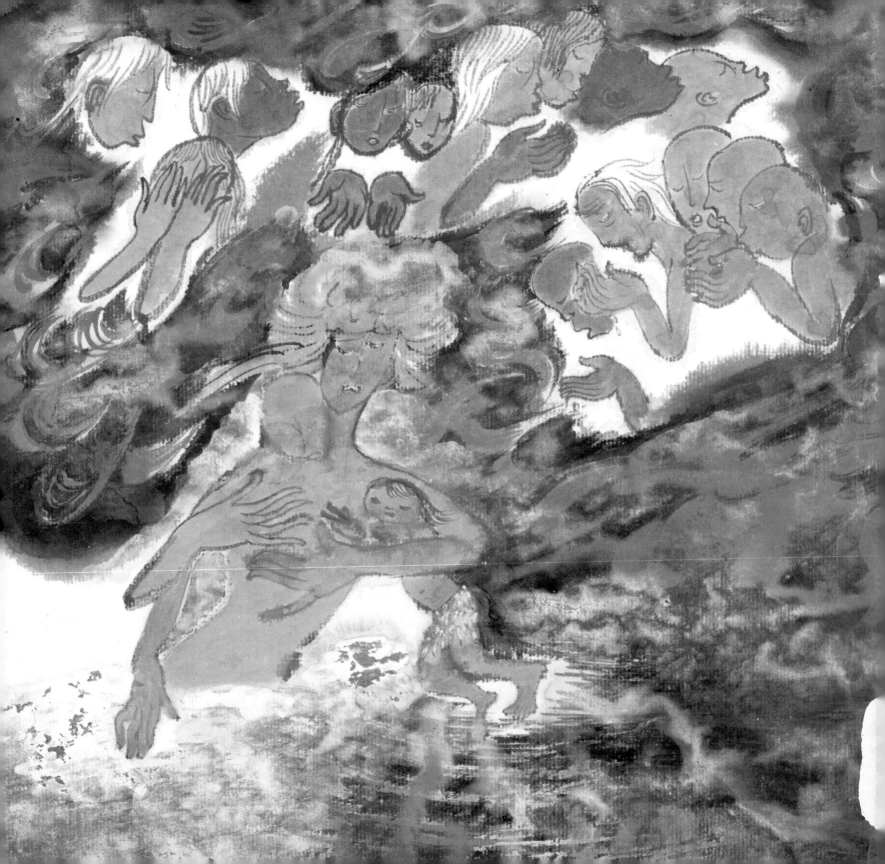

Mii's mother lifted Father onto her back again. She took Mii by the hand, and they began to run. Fire was moving toward them at a terrible speed. They ran among piles of cracked roof tiles, over fallen telephone poles and wires. Houses were burning on every side. They came to another river, and once in the water Mii felt suddenly sleepy. Before she knew it, she had gulped down mouthfuls of water. Her mother pulled her head above the water. They reached the other side and kept running.

At long last they reached the beach
outside Hiroshima. They could see Miyajima
island, wrapped in purple mist, across the
water. Mii's mother had hoped they could
cross over to the island by boat. Miyajima
was covered with beautiful pine and maple
trees and surrounded by clear water.
Thinking that safety was not far away, Mii
and her mother and father fell asleep.

The sun went down. Night came and went. The sun rose, then set. It rose and set again, then rose for the third time.

"Please, tell me what day it is," Mii's mother asked
a man who was passing by. He had been looking
over the people lying on the beach.

"It's the ninth," he answered.

Mother counted on her fingers. "Four days!"
she cried out in amazement. "We've been here
four days?"

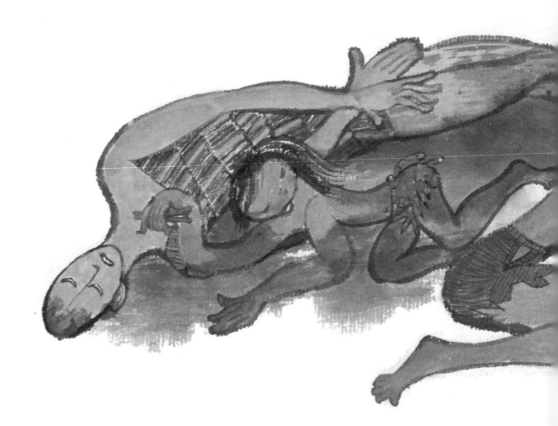

Mii started to cry softly. An old woman who was lying nearby sat up and took a rice ball out of her bag and gave it to Mii. When Mii took it from her, the woman fell down again. This time she didn't move.

"Mii-chan! You're still holding your chopsticks!" her mother exclaimed. "Here, let me have them." But Mii's hand wouldn't open. Her mother pried her fingers open one by one. Four days after the bomb, Mii let go of her chopsticks.

Firemen came from a nearby village to help them. Soldiers came and took the dead away. A school building that was still standing had been turned into a hospital, and they took Father there. There were no doctors, no medicine, no bandages—only shelter.

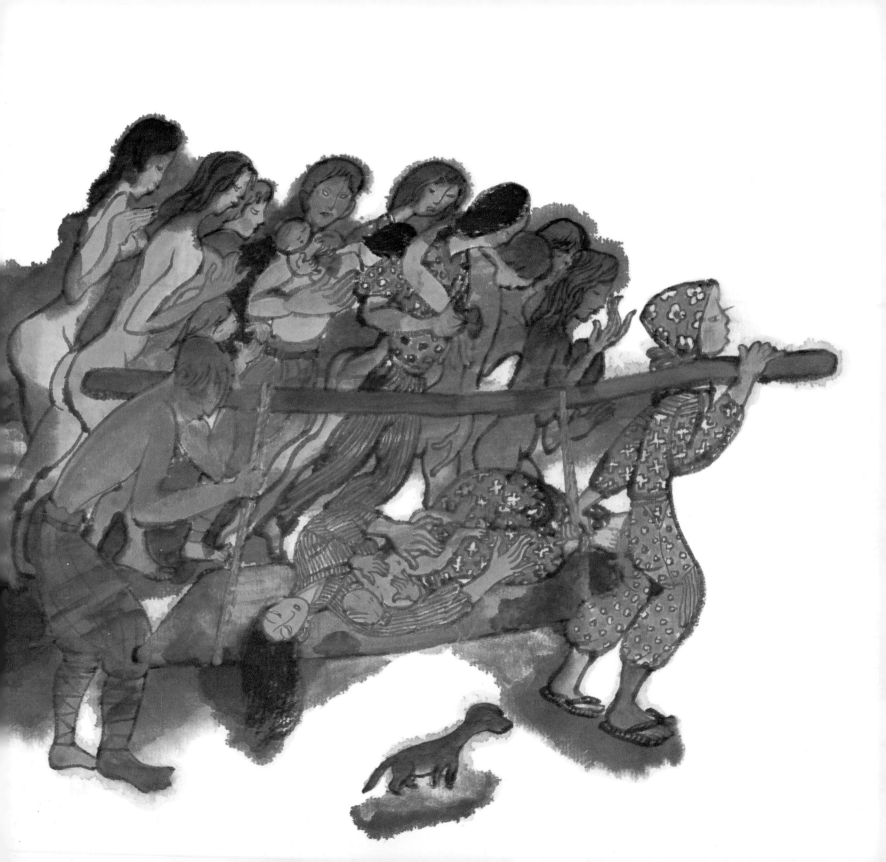

With Father as safe as possible in the hospital, Mii and her mother decided to go back into the city to see if anything was left of their home. There were neither grass nor trees nor houses left in Hiroshima. A burnt-out wasteland stretched before them as far as the eye could see. Mii and her mother found everything destroyed. The only thing left to remind them they had ever lived there was Mii's rice bowl. Bent and broken, it still contained some sweet potatoes.

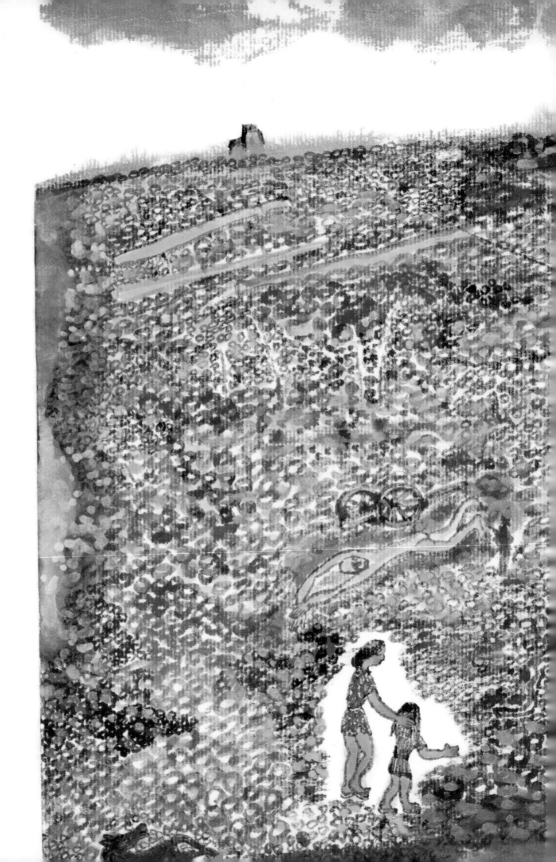

That day, August 9, 1945, as Mii and her mother looked at the rubble that had been Hiroshima, an atomic bomb was dropped on Nagasaki. And there, as in Hiroshima, thousands of people died, and anyone who survived was left homeless. Among the victims, in addition to the Japanese, were people from many other countries, such as Korea, China, Russia, Indonesia, and the United States.

The atomic bomb was unlike any explosive ever used before. The destruction on impact was greater than thousands of conventional bombs exploding all at once, and it also contaminated the area with radiation that caused deaths and illnesses for many years following the explosion.

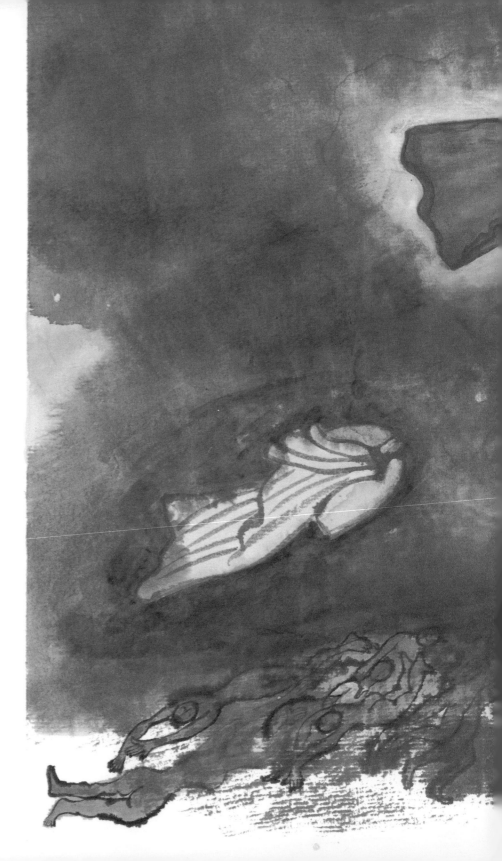

Mii never grew after that day. Many years have passed, and she is still the same size she was when she was seven years old. "It is because of the Flash from the bomb," her mother says. Sometimes Mii complains that her head itches, and her mother parts her hair, sees something shiny, and pulls it out of her scalp with a pair of tweezers. It's a sliver of glass, imbedded when the bomb went off years ago, that has worked its way to the surface.

Mii's father had seven wounds in his body, but they healed and for a while he thought he was getting well. Then one day in autumn after the Flash, his hair fell out and he began coughing blood. Purple spots appeared all over his body, and he died.

Many of the people who had said, "Thank God, our lives were spared," later became ill with radiation sickness. Though this happened in 1945, some of these people are still in hospitals. There is no cure for their disease.

Every year on August 6 the people of Hiroshima inscribe the names of loved ones who died because of the bomb on lanterns. The lanterns are lit and set adrift on the seven rivers that flow through Hiroshima. The rivers flow slowly to the sea, carrying the lanterns in memory of those who died.

Mii, who is still like a small child after all these years, writes "Father" on one lantern and "The Swallow" on another. Her mother's hair has now turned white, and she watches sorrowfully as her daughter sets the lanterns afloat.

"It can't happen again," she says, "if no one drops the bomb."

ABOUT THIS BOOK

In 1953 I was holding an exhibition of pictures about the atomic bomb, "Genbaku no Zu" in a small town in Hokkaido. Among the people at the exhibition I noticed a woman with a very angry expression on her face who stared at my pictures for a very long time. After a while she came out from the crowd and spoke to me.

"At first," she said, "I passed by your exhibit because I thought you were making a spectacle of suffering. I was determined not to come inside. But, now I am here and have seen your pictures. I want to tell you my story.

"After the Flash, I moved here to Hokkaido. The people of Hokkaido were not sympathetic or kind about my experiences. When I would speak of the Flash, they would say I was trying to draw upon their pity or that I was exaggerating my story. After a while, I didn't feel like telling anybody anything, so I never spoke of the Flash."

The woman closed her eyes after speaking. Then she reached for the microphone and began shouting into it: "You people who have come here, you will believe me. Please listen to me! Please believe me!" And, crying and choking over her words, she recounted the story of how she had tried to escape the Flash, carrying her wounded husband upon her back and leading her child by the hand. People listened to her. Some cried. When she had finished, she said simply, "Thank you for listening."

This scene remained with me for a long time, piercing my heart and memory. This book is based on that woman's story, but woven into it is all that I have heard and seen of other people's experiences with the atomic bomb.

*   *   *

I am now past seventy years old. I have neither children nor grandchildren. But I have written this book for grandchildren everywhere. It took me a very long time to complete it. It is very difficult to tell young people about something very bad that happened, in the hope that their knowing will help keep it from happening again. I thank my editors, the Chiba brothers, for their help and encouragement. I also thank my many good friends. And I wish to give special acknowledgment to Mr. Jitsuo Tabuchi, of Hiroshima City, and Mr. Kanji Kawade, public service manager of the Hiroshima Railway Company, who provided me with valuable materials.

—Toshi Maruki

Library of Congress Cataloging in Publication Data
Maruki, Toshi, (date)   Hiroshima no pika.   Translation of: Hiroshima no pika.
Summary: A retelling of a mother's account of what happened to her family during the
Flash that destroyed Hiroshima in 1945. 1. Hiroshima-shi (Japan)—Bombardment,
1945—Juvenile literature. 2. Atomic bomb—Japan—Hiroshima-shi—Juvenile literature.
3. World War, 1939-1945—Japan—Juvenile literature. 4. Japan—History—1912-1945—
Juvenile literature. [1. Hiroshima-shi (Japan)—Bombardment, 1945. 2. World War,
1939-1945—Japan. 3. Japan—History—1912-1945. 4. Atomic Bomb] I. Title.
D767.25.H6M2913   940.54'26   82-15365
ISBN 0-688-01297-3   AACR2